The Chronicles of Ms. Clarke's Class

Keep shining!

Julie Packett

Julie Packett

Illustrated by MacKenzie Fulmer

ISBN: 9781708190576

DEDICATION

This book is dedicated to any child who ever felt awkward in their skin or powerless to their fears. I, too, have felt that way as a child and even as an adult. However, great rewards have been gained when pushing through life struggles. I encourage you to give yourself the same pep talk you would give another. You're worth it.

CONTENTS

1 Classroom Duties

Julie

Each school year has a first day, a day where you meet new faces, spot familiar faces, and try not to make nervous faces. This year, I have Ms. Clarke, a teacher who likes to give all her work to her students. Last year's fifth graders said she assigns each student a classroom job. Some jobs are noble, like line leader, flag helper, or message carrier. I'm hoping I get germinator, the classroom's first line of defense against cooties, but I'll probably get a job that makes everyone hate me, like table monitor.

Who wants to tell their friends they can't talk during lunch? Not this girl!

The bell rings, and I head to my new classroom. Ms. Clarke, who is standing in front of the room, cheerfully says, "Good morning fifth graders. Are you ready for an exciting school year full of new experiences?"

She can't fool me. I know "new experiences" really means work, work, and more work.

I search each desk for my name and finally find it on a second row desk next to the window, the perfect spot. An envelope labeled "Classroom Duties" sits on my new desk. We all know what's coming next, she's about to assign us our jobs!

"Now class," says Ms. Clarke, "we are going to have a busy year, and I can use your help. In each envelope is a classroom duty that you will be responsible for each day. When I call your name, please come to the front of the class, share something about yourself, and tell us your classroom duty. Julie, you're up first."

I have to go first! I slowly stand and feel my knees buckle. I make my way to the front of the classroom and see 14 pairs of eyes staring at me, eagerly waiting to hear my horrible new job.

I softly say, "Hi. I'm Julie." I'm fiddling with my fingers and crinkling the envelope. I try to stop.

"Something about me?" I pause with all those eyes still glued to my face. "Well, I'm currently the hula hoop champion in my family."

A boy with orange hair interrupts, “How long can you hula?”

“My longest time is 37 seconds, but my little sister always tries to steal the hoop, so I know I can go longer. I can also hula hoop on my arm and foot,” I answer as my classmates let out a collective gasp of approval.

Ms. Clarke says, “That’s quite impressive, Julie. We would love to see you hula hoop one day.” I feel less nervous and somewhat proud. I almost forgot about the envelope in my hands.

I carefully open the envelope and pull out the note card. After a brief pause, I slowly read, “I’m the classroom weather reporter.”

“Excellent!” says Ms. Clarke. “That’s a very important job. We have an old weather station setup outside our school. You can see it from this window.” Ms. Clarke points past my desk to a pile of what looks like junk to me.

“It tracks temperature, wind speed and direction, and you can read the data from my computer. In addition, a rain gauge captures all the rain that has fallen in the past 24 hours. Your job, Julie, will be to read and empty the gauge each morning before coming into the classroom. I will also give you special permission to use my computer so you can get the current temperature and wind data too. We will start each class with your morning weather report of temperature, wind, and rainfall. Do you think you can handle that?”

I can’t tell Ms. Clarke no thanks, I’d rather be the classroom germinator. Weather reporter seems like quite a commitment. She expects me to get to school early every day just to see how much rain fell, and worse, speak in front of the class! Just thinking about reciting all those numbers in front of everyone makes me feel queasy.

2 First Impressions

Robbie

It's my first day at a new school, which is awesome because I get a fresh start. No one, including the teachers, know anything about my big brother, Daniel, and me.

I get off the bus right as the school bell rings, and I quickly head to my classroom. This year, I have Ms. Clarke. I know nothing about her, but I'm sure my charm and sense of humor will win her and all my classmates over today. I need to establish my presence on day one and show I'm not in anyone's shadow.

When I get to the classroom, all but one desk is taken. One boy looks like he isn't even awake yet and a girl with glasses is staring nervously at an envelope. In fact, all the desks have envelopes on them. Ms. Clarke is already rambling about the school year and gestures me to the only open desk, which has my name on it and is right in the front. Worst seat ever.

The nervous girl with glasses heads to the front of the class. She looks so scared; I could probably blow her over. She starts talking about how great of a hula hooper she is. I ask her how long she can hula. I bet I can go longer. I'll have to prove that in P.E.; that is sure to impress her and the other kids.

She opens up her envelope and says she's the weather reporter. What kind of school is this? Ms. Clarke is way too excited as she points to some rickety weather equipment out in the courtyard.

As our classroom weather reporter sits back down, Ms. Clarke looks right at me and says, “Alright Robbie, you’re up next. Come tell us a little about yourself.”

“No problem,” I say as I jump up from my desk and face the class.

“I’m Robbie. I’m really good at all sports. In fact, I want to be a sports announcer when I get older.” I point to the weather girl and say, “I have mad skills in hula hooping too.”

"That's nice, Robbie," Ms. Clarke interrupts. "You just moved here, right? Can you tell us about your previous town?"

"It was cold, real cold. I played ice hockey pretty much year around. The warmer weather here is a nice change, but I already miss the snow. We used to have epic snowball fights at recess," I say as I pretend to throw a snowball at the class.

"Well, it doesn't snow much here. Maybe once a year. We just live too close to the warm ocean," Ms. Clarke says. "Why don't you open your envelope and tell us your classroom duty?"

"Sure," I say as I rip it open. "I'm the teacher assistant." I can't help but squint my face in disappointment. "What does that mean?"

"I'm glad you asked," Ms. Clarke says with a smile. "Every morning you will take roll call and mark who is absent. I may also need you to help with miscellaneous tasks throughout the day, like stapling packets and putting them into homework folders."

"I don't mean to be rude, but don't you get paid to do that?" I ask. A few kids laugh, but most stay quiet. Ms. Clarke looks shocked. Oops.

"As I mentioned before," she says as she smiles again, "it's going to be a busy year, and I know you all can handle a little extra responsibility. You'll realize there are more lessons to be learned in life outside of routine school subjects. I think you'll find this is a very important job with great personal rewards."

I know this isn't the time to say I'll pass, and I'd rather be the classroom commentator, giving a play-by-play of all the action throughout the school day.

Maybe I didn't make the best first impression on day one.

3 Weather or Not

Julie

At dinner, I sit quietly. “How was your first day of school, Julie?” Mom asks.

“It was fine,” I say as I scooch peas back and forth on my plate.

“How’s your new teacher?” Dad asks.

I can feel my eyes start to water, and my throat tightens. I try to keep my emotions bottled inside, but even Clara, my little sister, can tell something is wrong. Everyone is quiet and looking at me. Is this how it’s going to be each morning at school? Everyone waiting for knowledge to come out of my mouth, and I can't make a sound?

As the tears stream down my face, I mutter, "I'm the classroom weather reporter. I have to stand in front of the class and tell them a bunch of weather facts each morning."

"That sounds exciting, honey," Mom says as she tries to comfort me. "You'll make a great meteorologist."

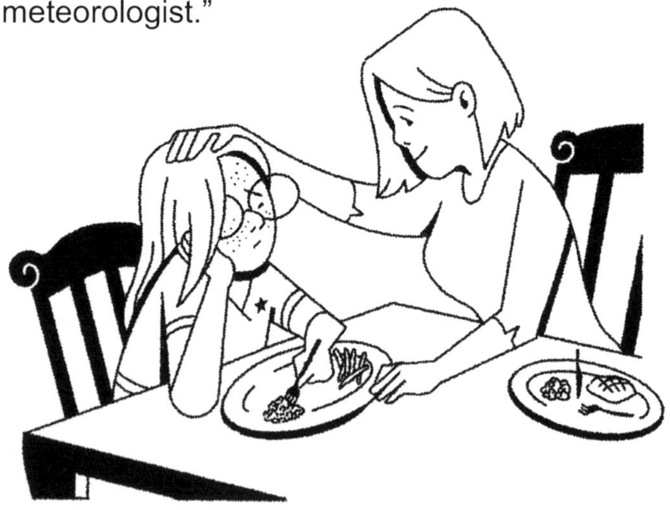

"What's a mee-tee...whatever that word you just said?" asks Clara.

"Mee-tee-ur-aa-luh-juhst," Mom says while moving her mouth in all sorts of weird ways, stretching out each sound. "It's a person who studies the weather." She turns back to me and says, "You love watching the clouds and hearing thunder roar. You even start counting every time you see lightning."

"It's just the five second rule, Mom. I just want to know how far the storm is from us," I mumble.

"What's the five second rule?" Clara says while rubbing her head as if it hurts.

"You can tell how far away the lightning is by counting the seconds between seeing the flash of lightning and when you hear thunder. The lightning is about a mile away if you count five seconds, about two miles if you count ten seconds. Get it?" I confidently say to my sister.

"Oh, yes. I get it." Clara says with a confused look on her face.

"Look at you! You're already teaching others," Mom says with a smile. "Now you'll get to learn more about weather and share it with your classmates. Your father and I can help you prepare so you feel more comfortable." Mom turns to Dad, "Honey, a little help here. Don't we have an old rain gauge we can set up in the backyard?"

"Oh yeah. I'm sure I can find it," Dad says.

"I wouldn't mind knowing how much it rains in our backyard," says Mom. "That knowledge might help me with my garden."

Their excitement makes me think that maybe this isn't going to be such a bad job after all. As I wipe my eyes, I ask, "Do you think we can set up the rain gauge tonight? I have to give my first report tomorrow morning."

"Of course, we will set it up right after dinner. Rain is in the forecast tonight too. We can check the gauge in the morning before you leave for school so you can get a little practice. Now, finish those peas before they roll right off your plate," Dad says.

I haven't even made my first observation, and I already feel better. With my parent's help, I'm going to be the best weather reporter in 5B history!

4 Strategic Planning

Robbie

The first day of school didn't quite go as planned. Sure, I made some new friends, but I need to work on my strategy for day two. After the bus dropped me off at home, I quickly ran past my grandma and headed to my bedroom, shut the door, and started brainstorming. Thankfully, my brother doesn't get home for a little while.

I pull out a pencil and paper and write, "Operation Fifth Grade Take Over: Day 2" and start the list with "bus ride." Sometimes the person you sit next to doesn't want to talk. I'll make sure I get a window seat so they have to look over my shoulder to see outside. It would be rude to hover over someone and not talk to them.

Next, I add "lots of jokes" to the list. I need some jokes ready to go for those awkward, quiet moments during class. I'm sure Ms. Clarke will appreciate the distraction.

I follow jokes with "great lunch." Everyone always checks out each other's lunches, and a peanut butter and honey sandwich just doesn't spark much interest from the other kids.

Last, I write down "trade job." Being the teacher assistant doesn't show off my talents. I need a job that puts me front and center. Tomorrow I'll have to do some more research on the different classroom jobs and see who would be interested in trading.

Just then, I hear my brother get home. He's already telling Grandma how great his first day was, how everyone loves him, and how the football coach wants him to try out for the team. I roll my eyes and just hope he doesn't come to my room.

Bang, bang, bang. He swings open my bedroom door and immediately starts messing up my hair. "Hey bro, what are you working on?" he asks.

"Nothing, go away," I say as I flip my paper over. "It's just homework."

"Homework on the first day? I guess fifth grade is tougher than tenth," he says. "Well, finish that later, Grandma wants us to run to the store and grab a few things for dinner."

As much as I would rather stay home and work on my list, this will give me a chance to find something interesting for lunch. "Fine," I say as I grab my football. He may be a showoff, but at least he'll throw the ball with me as we walk to the store.

5 First Day on the Job

Julie

It's a cloudy but comfortable morning. The ground is wet, and the toads are happy, croaking and jumping in puddles. Dad and I measured 0.53 inches of rain in our gauge this morning. As I walk to school, I wonder what the school gauge will show. "Do you think it rained more or less at school?" I ask Dad.

"We live so close to school, but I'll guess more," Clara says as she kicks a wet pinecone down the sidewalk.

"Hmm, I'm not sure," Dad answers. "There seems to be more puddles as we get closer, so I'll go with Clara's guess of more." Clara proudly smiles up at Dad as he squeezes both our hands. "What do you think?"

"I need more information before I make my prediction," I say as I adjust my glasses.

"Spoken like a true meteorologist," Dad teases.

As we drop Clara off at her classroom, Dad continues to walk with me to the school rain gauge. There are a few students in the courtyard, but it's otherwise quiet.

"Would you look at that? They have the same rain gauge as us," Dad says. "Alright, what's your reading?"

I peek at the water level inside the measuring tube. “I think it reads 0.97 inches. Is that right?” I ask.

My dad gives it a look. “Sure is!” he proudly verifies. “Now what do you do?”

“I pour out the rain water and log the total on Ms. Clarke’s computer,” I say. “She said she will help me get the temperature and wind information.”

I give Dad a hug and dash into the building. Ms. Clarke smiles as I walk into the classroom. “Good morning, Julie. I saw you outside with your father. How much rain was in the gauge?”

“0.97 inches,” I answer. “Where should I log it?”

Ms. Clarke shows me how to enter the data into her computer. As I’m typing in the last bit of information, the bell rings. Kids come streaming into the classroom, and butterflies immediately start swarming in my stomach. I completely forgot that I have to talk in front of my class. How could I forget such a thing?

"Class, take a seat. Julie is just about to present her first morning weather report," says Ms. Clarke.

"I can give a weather report," smirks Robbie. "It rained last night, and it's cloudy." Everyone giggles, and for some reason I can't explain, I feel embarrassed.

"Thank you for stating the obvious, Robbie, but Julie will provide you with a little more information than that," Ms. Clarke claps back. "Julie, come share your weather knowledge with the rest of us."

I stand up from Ms. Clarke's chair and make my way, again, to the front of the classroom. After clearing my throat, I say, "Yes, it rained, but the neat thing is how much it rained at school compared to my house." I pause as bored faces stare at me.

Despite my nerves, I continue, "You see, I live just three blocks away from the school, and last night my dad and I set up a rain gauge at my house before the rain started. This morning, I took a rainfall report at my house and then at school. Even though I live close, nearly twice as much rain fell at school. To be exact, 0.53 inches fell at my house, and 0.97 inches fell at school."

Ms. Clarke interrupts, "That's fantastic, Julie! I've never had a weather reporter take observations at two different locations. Class, Julie is providing you with a great lesson on rainfall variability. I suggest you pay close attention to her morning reports."

My classmates' bored faces morph to impressed expressions. Did I just become the best 5B weather reporter on the second day of school?

6 Recess Agreement

Robbie

After Julie's weather report, I realize that I should be the one entertaining the class first thing in the morning, not taking boring roll call. There are so many weather jokes I could tell.

Knock, knock.

Who's there?

Wet.

Wet who?

Wet me in, it's raining out here!

That would have been the perfect opener to today's report.

At recess, I spot Julie on the swings. As I head towards her, Mary Sue stops me. It's only my second day at this school, but I can already tell she's a goody two-shoes who thinks she runs it.

"Robbie, right? I'm Mary Sue. How do you do?" she says.

"Yeah, I'm fine," I say as I try to walk away.

She grabs my arm and says, "I'd like to make you an offer. How would you like to be the class germinator?"

"You don't want to be it?" I ask while keeping my eyes on Julie. I can't lose sight of her. Once the bell rings, everyone rushes inside, and she doesn't sit next to me in class.

"Do I look like someone who wants to be a germinator?" she says with a disgusted look on her face.

"I'm not sure what a germinator looks like," I say.

"Well," she says, "they don't look like me. I'm meant to be the teacher assistant, in charge of schedules, grades, awards, things like that."

"You do realize I just take roll call and staple papers, right?" I ask.

"Just right now that's all you do," she says with a smirk, "but there is so much more potential for the teacher's assistant than the class germinator. I bet by the end of the year you could be on a first name basis with Ms. Clarke."

"No thanks," I say. "I'm planning to ask Julie to trade with me."

“You want to be the weather reporter?” she asks while looking at Julie. “Why?”

“Because the weather reporter gets to put on a show for two minutes each morning. All eyes would be on me,” I explain.

Mary Sue taps her forehead as if that will help her brain problem solve faster. Finally, she says, “How about we include Julie in this trade? You get to be the weather reporter, Julie can be the germinator, and I’ll be the wonderful and adorable teacher assistant.”

“I’m fine with that, but this only works if we can get Julie to agree to make the switch,” I say. I then notice Julie has caught both of us looking at her. It’s time to make our move.

7 Job Trading

Julie

As the school day rolls on, I realize all my classmates, even ones I've never met, know my name. I feel a confidence I've never felt before at school. Yes, I rule the upstairs at home, but I've never commanded that same authority at school. Who knew being the classroom weather reporter would have such a fan base.

At recess, Gracy and I are trying to swing in sync when I spot Mary Sue and Robbie whispering and pointing at me. It doesn't take a great detective to know that I'm their topic of conversation. Once they realize they've been busted, they start walking towards us. Gracy, who is oblivious to what has just transpired, keeps rambling on and on about her latest crush. Her voice fades as my palms start to sweat. What would Mary Sue and Robbie want from me? I don't even know Robbie, and Mary Sue normally acts as if she doesn't even recognize me even though we've been in the same school for years.

"Julie," Mary Sue says with a smile, "Robbie and I would like to make you an offer." I stop pumping my legs so my swing slows down. Robbie keeps shifting his eyes back and forth between Mary Sue and me.

"That's right," Robbie adds. "This is important."

Gracy and I hop off our swings and both stick our landings. We've been attached at the hip since first grade, but for some reason we aren't in the same class this year. It's as if Principal Diaz didn't get my memo. At least we get recess together. "What do you two want?" Gracy protectively questions.

"It's about our classroom job duties," Mary Sue says while putting her hands on her hips. "Robbie got teacher assistant, and I got germinator. I'm not interested in squirting clear goo onto a bunch of dirty hands."

"And I'm not interested in being the teacher's pet, not now, not ever," Robbie proudly declares.

Mary Sue rolls her eyes and turns to Robbie. "Teacher assistant doesn't mean you're the teacher's pet. It means you're second in charge." She looks back at Gracy and me. "And we all know, I'm the best for that position," she boasts.

I nervously put my hands in my pockets and suggest they just switch jobs. "I'm sure Ms. Clarke will let you two trade. What do you need from me?"

"I want to be the weather whiz kid of 5B, and I won't give teacher assistant to Mary Sue unless you join our trade," Robbie declares. "I was born to talk in front of the class. I could come up with so many weather jokes. Wouldn't you rather be the classroom germinator?"

"Whoa," says Gracy while throwing her hands up. "I hear that Julie gave an awesome weather report this morning. Tell em' Jules."

I like to think no one notices I'm nervous, that somehow I hide it just enough to where they think I choose to be quiet, but Gracy is right. I felt great after my morning weather report. On the other hand, I originally wanted germinator. All these thoughts go through my mind within seconds; meanwhile, Mary Sue and Robbie are staring at me, waiting for me to accept their offer.

As I look down at the ground, I say quietly, "No thanks."

Robbie can't believe his ears. "What? Come on, you know I'm made for this!"

I lift my head, and Mary Sue and Robbie look shocked. Gracy has her arm around me and is proudly smiling back at them. "I appreciate the offer," I say, "but I'll keep my job. I think I'm starting to like it."

The bell rings, and Mary Sue and Robbie take off toward the school building. As they run, Robbie yell's back, "Let us know if you change your mind."

Gracy grabs both my shoulders and looks me dead in the eyes. "I'm proud of you, Jules. You make a great weather girl. Don't let those knuckleheads talk you into switching if you don't want to."

I take a deep breath and realize how glad I am that I didn't trade. Sure, germinator would be an easy, respectable job that doesn't make me the center of attention every day, but maybe I'm starting to secretly like being center stage.

8 Teacher Assistant

Robbie

As the school day rolls on, I keep trying to make eye contact with Julie, but she just remains focused on her classwork. Just as I'm about to throw a wad of paper her way, Ms. Clarke asks me to come to her desk. As I get up, paper still in hand, I notice Mary Sue watching my every step.

"Robbie, I know you were just about to lob that snowball across the room," she quietly says, "but I need you to do something for me first."

I slowly slip the ball of paper into my back pocket as if she didn't just call me out.

"I need you to go to the front office and ask them to make 20 copies of this," she says as she hands me a piece of paper. "Take your lunch box with you because once you have the copies, you can meet us in the cafeteria. Do you think you can handle that?"

"Of course," I confidently say.

I grab my lunch box and head toward the door with Mary Sue's eyes still glued to me. As I walk down the quiet hall, I realize maybe this teacher assistant job isn't so bad after all.

After I complete my duties, I head to the cafeteria with 20 copies in hand. I hand them to Ms. Clarke and find a seat next to Julie. Time to show off my new lunch items.

“Hey Julie, care to see what’s in my lunch box?” I say while waving my hands around like I’m about to do a magic trick.

“No thanks,” she says as she shifts her body away from me.

I continue anyways by pulling out a cheese stick and saying, “What do you call cheese that isn’t yours?”

She just shrugs.

“Nacho cheese!” I exclaim as she cracks a smile.

I know I have to step it up so I say, “Why did the fisherman put peanut butter into the sea?”

“To go with the jellyfish,” she quietly says as she turns back toward me.

We both laugh as I take out my sandwich cut in the shape of a fish.

Even though I would make an awesome weather reporter, I think I’ll stop asking her to trade, at least for now.

9 An Exciting Announcement

Julie

After lunch, Ms. Clarke tells us to quickly take a seat as she has an exciting announcement. We all dash to our desks full of anticipation. My mind starts wondering what the news could possibly be. Maybe we're going on a field trip, having a guest speaker, or getting a classroom pet. Yes, a classroom pet would truly be an exciting announcement.

"Now class, I know it's just the second day of school, but I've already told you that this is going to be a busy year full of new lessons and adventures," Ms. Clarke says with a smile.

Could we actually be getting a classroom pet? Caring for an animal will teach us many lessons and will surely be adventurous, especially if the pet is something exotic, like a bearded dragon.

Robbie's hand shoots up. "Are we putting on a play? I'd be happy to be the lead," he proudly boasts.

"Robbie, thank you for raising your hand, but wait to speak until I call your name," scolds Ms. Clarke. "We aren't putting on a play, but there will be other opportunities throughout the year for you to showcase your showmanship talents."

She winks at Robbie as he pumps his fist with excitement. I sink into my chair.

"Over the next couple of weeks, you are all going to complete a science project and display your work to all your peers and parents during Science Night. You can come up with your own topic or take one from this list I'm handing out," she says.

I sink into my chair some more.

"Be as creative as you want. Just be prepared for questions as there will be three judges selecting the winners," she adds.

It's clear to me that Ms. Clarke has no clue what an "exciting announcement" really means. Not only are we not getting a classroom pet, but I have to present a science project in front of everyone.

I look out the window and realize it's starting to rain. I focus on the raindrops hitting the swings.

Drip, drop, drip.

A flash of lightning brings me out of my trance, and I immediately start counting to myself, “one, two, three, four, five, six, seven, eight, nine.” A deep rumble of thunder interrupts my counting, almost ten seconds. The lightning is about two miles away.

Drip, drop, drip.

Maybe presenting a science project won’t be so bad. I should come up with a topic that interests me.

Drip, drop, drip.

I’ll have rain to measure tomorrow morning. I wonder if my measurements between home and school will be different again.

Drip, drop, drip.

That’s it!

10 Science Project

Robbie

As Ms. Clarke explains all the science fair project requirements, I immediately start trying to figure out a project idea that will win me first place. I obviously can't use a topic off her list. I have to come up with my own creative topic that will wow the judges. If one of the judges is Mr. Robertson, the school librarian, I know I can win him over with cats. He loves cats. It's obvious by all the cat posters in the library. If a judge is Ms. Jackson, our P.E. teacher, I bet she would be drawn to a sports topic.

I raise my hand and fight every urge to just start talking.

"Yes, Robbie," Ms. Clarke says as she points to me.

"Who are the three judges?" I ask.

"That's a good question, but they will remain anonymous until Science Night," Ms. Clarke says.

Strike one. I raise my hand again.

"Yes, Robbie," Ms. Clarke says again.

"Can we work with a partner or in groups?" I ask. "I would be the perfect presenter while another person could be the number cruncher."

“No, this is a solo project, but you can enlist the help of your family members,” she says. “You can also come to me for additional support, if needed.”

Strike two. I raise my hand up, again. “Last question, I promise,” I say.

“Go ahead, Robbie,” she says with a patient smile.

“Do you need an announcer for Science Night?” I put my hand on my ear and do my best news anchor voice, “Introducing judge number one, she likes long walks on the beach and…”

Ms. Clarke interrupts my brilliant impression and says, “Thank you for the offer, but Principal Diaz and I will host Science Night.”

Strike three. I’m down for the count. Maybe Daniel can help me come up with a ribbon winning idea. I’m sure he got first place in his last science fair.

11 Weather Whiz Kid

Julie

Finally, the school bell rings, and I rush to the bus loop. I can't wait to tell Gracy about my science fair project. Gracy wants to be a veterinarian so I'm sure she will do something with animals. As I move through the crowd, I hear Robbie telling other kids that he's planning to win first place at Science Night even though he doesn't have a topic yet.

I spot Gracy talking to a girl in my class named Sadie and dash towards them. "Gracy!" I holler, "did your teacher tell you about Science Night?"

"Sure did! Sadie and I were just talking about it. I have the perfect topic," she says with her hands up in the air. "Are you ready to hear it?"

"Of course," I say.

"Do dogs prefer a certain color bowl when eating?" she says.

"Nice!" I exclaim.

"I already have to feed our three dogs every day. Might as well make an experiment out of it," she adds. "What about you?"

"I'm going to continue to track the rainfall at my house and compare it to the rain that falls at the school. It's called rainfall variability or something like that. Maybe I'll notice a pattern."

"Introducing Weather Whiz Kid Julie!" Gracy announces to the bus crowd as Sadie circles her hands around her mouth and mimics a cheering crowd.

I give my best superhero pose and flash a big smile. The wind even picks up and makes my hair fly. Finally, all that nervous, new school year energy is gone.

“I couldn’t help overhearing,” Mary Sue interrupts, “but now you really aren’t going to trade jobs with Robbie and me, are you?” she groans.

“Nope. I’m on a raindrop mission,” I proudly say.

Gracy and I do our very cool, best friend hand shake before I turn and head to the front of the school where my mom meets Clara and me. I need to get home and start working on my weather game plan. How will I handle observations over the weekend? Maybe Dad will still walk up to the school with me after breakfast on Saturday and Sunday. I have to keep my observations consistent. The science fair blue ribbon is on the line.

Even as I get further away from the bus loop, I can still feel Mary Sue's eyes on the back of my head. I make sure to add a little more pep in my step.

12 Bus Ride Discoveries

Robbie

While waiting for my bus to arrive, Mary Sue huffs, puffs, and marches towards me. “Robbie!” she yells while being ten yards still out. “Robbie, we need to talk!” she yells some more.

“Well hey, Mary Sue. Having a good afternoon?” I sarcastically ask.

“Very funny,” she smirks. “Julie isn’t going to trade with us. I’m stuck being the germinator.”

“I kind of figured that out when she told us no during recess,” I say.

Just then, my bus arrives. "Oh darn. I wish I could stay and chat about this some more, Mary Sue, but I have a bus to catch. Let's wallow about this tomorrow," I say as she glares at me.

I hop on the bus first and grab a window seat. A boy from my class named Emilio sits beside me.

"That was hilarious, man," he says.

"What was hilarious?" I ask.

He points out the window at Mary Sue. "Her face is so red it looks like steam is going to start shooting out of her ears. She can't believe she isn't going to get her way," he says.

We talk the entire ride. He points out different areas around town, from the best place to get an ice cream float to the best parks and why.

Once I get home, I help Grandma make dinner, meatloaf again. I find myself talking about how much I like helping Ms. Clarke.

“I guess I really don’t mind being the teacher assistant,” I say.

“Well, you’ve been a great helper around here for me,” Grandma points out.

At dinner, Daniel can’t stop talking about his first day at football tryouts. Grandma just stares at him with such pride. Somehow, I need to make my way into this conversation.

“Hey Daniel,” I interrupt, “my friend Emilio told me there’s a park a few blocks away that used to be the high school's football field. They still have a goal post there.”

“Awesome!” he says. “I’ll have to take my buddies there sometime.”

Grandma looks at me and says, “Robbie, why don’t you tell your brother about your science project idea.”

I’m never nervous at school or with my friends, but for some reason, I always find myself hesitating around Daniel. Grandma gives me an encouraging nod.

“Well,” I say, “with the field goal post just up the street, I think it would be fun to see how distance impacts accuracy.”

“That’s cool,” he says. “My fifth grade science project was boring. Do different food colored ice cubes thaw at varying rates? News flash, they don’t,” he says.

Grandma and I lock eyes. She squints at me and says, “Isn’t there more, Robbie?”

“Yes,” I say squinting my eyes back at her. “I’ll log the results of four kicks from the 10 yard line. I’ll do the same from the 20, 30, 40, and 50 yard line.”

“Sounds like a great idea,” Daniel says while stealing a piece of meatloaf off Grandma’s plate and shoving it into his mouth.

“Do you think you could help me figure out the results? I need a kicker,” I say.

“Sure, I’ll be your kicker,” he says. “Why didn’t you just say that in the beginning?”

“I just figured you’d be too busy,” I quietly say.

“Robbie, I’ve already told you,” he says, “I know I seem busy, but I’m always here for you, bro.”

13 Game Plan

Julie

As we walk home, I can't help but ramble on and on to my mom about Science Night and my project. Clara keeps trying to interrupt, but my excitement overshadows her attempts.

"Ms. Clarke says we have to come up with a question and form a hy…hypot....hypotumus, an informed guess to that question," I say.

"You mean hypothesis," Mom says.

“Yes, hypothesis,” I repeat. “My question for my project is what causes rainfall variability between my house and school?”

“Oh my, variability another big word,” Mom says with a smile.

“Ms. Clarke said that after my report this morning. She was impressed that I compared rainfall at our house to the school. Based on her reaction, I think I already have her vote for that blue ribbon.” I proudly say. “But that got me thinking, why did it rain so much more at school? We only live a few blocks away.”

Finally, Clara throws her hands up in frustration and blocks the sidewalk. “How can I help?” she asks.

Although she’s only in first grade, she's smart and loves her big sister. She always wants to be involved in anything I do. Most of the time it’s great, but when Gracy spends the night, we can’t get her to leave us alone. She always wants to pretend we're cats. She insists on wearing cat ears every day. Mom says it's just a phase.

"Well, this is a big project, and I really want to win first place; therefore, I'll take all the help I can get. I'm sure I can find something for you to do," I say.

"Thank you," she says as she turns and proudly marches down the sidewalk.

"Would you like to be the one that pours the water out each morning?" I ask her.

Clara turns back around with her hands on her hips. She squints her eyes at me as if she thinks I'm trying to trick her. "That doesn't sound very important," she proclaims.

"Of course it is, honey," Mom says as she strokes Clara's blonde hair. "It's one of the most important parts of the entire process."

"If we don't pour out the water after every observation, the reading the next day will be wrong, and the day after that, and the day after that," I add.

Clara shrugs her shoulders and crosses her arms as if she's not convinced.

"Would you rather be my photographer?" I ask.

Clara loves taking pictures with my parents' phones. They are always finding photos of her dolls, our pets, and loads of close-ups of Clara's face. "The selfie monster strikes again!" Dad always jokes.

"I need plenty of pictures of me taking observations for my poster. 20 percent of my grade is based on my poster alone. If I have lots of great photos, I feel like my chances for winning goes up," I add.

"That's a great idea. Julie can't take pictures of herself if she's pouring out the rain gauge. What do you say, Clara?" Mom asks.

"That does sound pretty important," Clara says as she uncrosses her arms. I can see her first grade brain working overtime as she weighs her options. "Can my name be added to the poster, 'photos by Clara'?" she asks.

"Of course!" I say as I put my arm around her. "You'd be doing me a favor. But you will have to come with Dad and me to the school this weekend and take pictures of me with the school rain gauge," I say.

"You have a deal. That sounds like the purrr-fect job for me," she says with a big smile and as she turns to march home.

After dinner, my dad helps me create a spreadsheet on his computer so we can keep track of all the daily observations. I would rather just write them down, but my dad insists having the information printed on a chart will look nicer on my poster.

“Can you think of anything else we should include?” Dad asks.

So far, I have columns labeled with the day of the week, house rainfall, and school rainfall.

“I should add a note about how there were more puddles at school than at home,” I say.

“That’s a great idea,” he says.

Meanwhile, Clara takes about 30 pictures of me as I awkwardly enter this morning’s totals into the spreadsheet. Thankfully, I still have 13 more days to become more comfortable with this computer. Maybe she’ll get a better picture of me next week.

14 Ask a Question

Robbie

It's day three of school, and thankfully my bus arrived on time this morning. As I walk into the classroom, Ms. Clarke is writing our morning assignment on the whiteboard, and Julie is entering weather information into Ms. Clarke's computer.

"Hey Julie," I holler across the classroom, "what happens when it rains cats and dogs?"

"I don't know, what?" she asks.

"You have to be careful not to step in a poodle!" I exclaim. We both laugh, and even Ms. Clarke lets out a small chuckle.

"Good one," she replies. "I'll make sure to tell that to my dad." I flinch, and she pretends to not notice. It's just an automatic response when someone says dad.

Just then, the bell rings and kids stream into the classroom. Mary Sue glares at me as I head to Ms. Clarke's podium. "Class, please take your seats," I loudly say while smiling at Mary Sue.

After roll call and Julie's weather report, Ms. Clarke points to the whiteboard in the front of the class. "Ask a Question" is written in big letters.

"Alright scientists," Ms. Clarke says, "over the next two weeks, I'm going to ask for updates on the status of your science project to encourage you to not wait until the last minute to start it. Today, I want you to simply write the question you hope to answer by doing research and conducting an experiment."

Mary Sue raises her hand.

"Yes, Mary Sue," Ms. Clarke says.

"What if we don't know what we want to do yet?" she asks.

"That's okay for now," answers Ms. Clarke, "just write down that you don't have a topic on a sheet of paper, but make sure you brainstorm ideas tonight."

I pull out a blank sheet from my notebook and look around the classroom to check out my competition. Mary Sue, who sits beside me, quickly writes "no question yet" on her paper. Emilio, who sits behind me, is just staring at his blank paper. So far, I'm not worried.

I look to my left and see a girl named Sadie already answering her question, and Julie vigorously writing while biting her lower lip. Intense.

I turn back to my paper and write, "Does distance from a field goal affect kick accuracy?" I realize that even though I really want to win first place, I'm more excited that Daniel and I will be hanging out again.

15 Weekend Weather

Julie

For the rest of the school week, I check the rainfall at both my house and school as a six-year-old documents every moment. “Julie, look this way,” Clara demands. Click. “Over here, Julie.” Click. “Can you pour the water out slower?” Click.

Each night, Dad helps me enter my observations into the spreadsheet on his computer. I add as many notes as I can, like whether the ground was soggy or dry, if the ditches were full or empty, or if the plants look waterlogged or wilted. Click, flash.

It is finally Saturday, and Dad and I walk to the school for my fifth day of observations. Clara has taken a break from her photography duties to watch Saturday morning cartoons. I don't mind because it gives me some time to chat with him without Clara interrupting us.

"Dad, over the last couple of days, I've noticed that the amount of rain is always different between the school and our house, even though we live so close," I say. "I've been trying to figure out why."

"Well," Dad says, "maybe we need more information. Just knowing how much rain fell is just one piece of the equation. We can watch the morning weather report on TV before walking to school each morning, and if it does rain, we can look at the radar to see which way the storms are moving. When we get back home, we can flip on the TV. How does that sound?"

"Sounds like a plan," I say as I try to step in sync with him. "That will help me make my morning reports even more exciting."

"How are your reports going?" he asks as he purposely takes smaller steps so I can match his stride.

"I've gotten better," I say. "In fact, Ms. Clarke even mentioned she's proud of my growing confidence. I'm assuming that's a compliment."

"It sure is," he says as he squeezes my hand.

"Oh, I have a joke for you. What happens when it rains cats and dogs?" I ask.

"You got me," he says.

"You step in a poodle," I answer as we both laugh our same shoulder shrug laugh. "A new boy at school told me that joke."

"Oh, yeah. What's his name?" he asks.

"Robbie," I say. "He moved here from someplace cold, like ice hockey cold."

"Not much ice hockey around here," he says.

"At first I didn't think I was going to like him. He tried to switch classroom jobs with me," I say.

"No way," he gasps jokingly.

"But I told him no, and he hasn't bothered me about it again. He's actually really nice," I say.

"And tells great jokes," he adds.

16 Operation: Field Goal Kick

Robbie

It's finally the weekend! Grandma and I attempt to make football shaped pancakes in honor of Operation: Field Goal Kick.

"Do you think Daniel will be up soon?" I ask.

"That teenage boy will be down any minute now. He can't resist the smell of hot pancakes and bacon. Neither can you," Grandma says as she gives me a side hug. "I'm glad you boys will get a little time together today."

"Me too," I say while making the perfect pancake flip in the pan.

“10 out of 10! You’re quite the chef,” she proudly exclaims.

After a brief silence, I ask, “Grandma, do you think he blames me?”

She grabs both my shoulders, stares straight into my eyes, and sternly says, “Absolutely not.”

I shrug loose of her grasp so I can flip another pancake. “He just keeps so busy. It’s like he’s avoiding me or something,” I explain.

"You know, Love," she says as she turns the sizzling bacon, "about thirty years ago when your grandpa died, I found myself widowed, raising two young boys in this very house." She points upstairs and adds, "In those exact rooms."

"I know," I say. "I'm in Uncle Robert's room."

"You sure are," she says, "and Daniel is in your father's room. Although it was tough for many years, we were a tight trio, just like you and Daniel were with your father after your mother passed away. I learned a lot about football and cars back then, which is coming in handy these days." She gives me a little side hip bump.

"You probably know more football stats than any other grandma," I say while returning the bump.

"You just need to talk to your brother. I'm sure he doesn't realize how you feel," she says.

I hug her, and she squeezes me tight. I take a deep breath, and her powdery scent fills my lungs.

“Everyone copes with loss differently,” she adds, “and he is distracting himself with extra school activities right now. It doesn’t mean he loves you any less.”

She slowly lets go of me and pulls out three plates from the cabinet. I add pancakes and bacon to each, and as she turns to pour orange juice into glasses, I add extra bacon to my plate.

“I know he loves me,” I say, “I just feel like he doesn’t like me anymore.”

“Impossible. You’re the one that keeps everyone laughing in this house,” she says with a smile.

Just then, Daniel comes sprinting down the stairs. “I smell breakfast,” he proclaims.

"Your brother made football shaped pancakes and bacon," says Grandma.

"Nice! Thanks bro," he says as he messes up my hair. "Ready for today?"

"Yup, I have everything we need packed: football, kicking tee, notebook, camera, and snacks," I say.

"Can't forget the snacks," he jokes while taking a big bite of pancake.

17 What's a Sea Breeze?

Julie

"Clara, I need to change the channel," I say. "Dad and I want to watch the morning news."

"But this is my favorite part," she whines.

"Spoiler alert, the good guys win," I say as I pick up the remote. "Besides, I only need a few minutes to check out the morning weather report."

I flip the channel, and just as expected, our local weather reporter is showing a map of the expected high temperatures for the day. "It's another hot one with highs in the 90s," she says as she gestures with her hands, "but just like yesterday, if you are heading out in the afternoon, remember to pack an umbrella as the sea breeze will bring showers and thunderstorms to the area later today."

"Dad," I yell, "what's a sea breeze?"

Dad strolls into the living room sipping on his second cup of coffee.

"Ah, the sea breeze," he says. "Let's look it up on the internet after you enter this morning's observations."

"See, all done, Clara," I say as I toss her the remote and run to the computer.

I turn it on and pull up my spreadsheet. I enter 0.28 inches under the home column and 0.73 under the school column. Then I pull up a search engine and type, "what is a sea breeze" into the search box. This internet thing is really smart and quickly gives me an answer. I turn to Dad and joke, "Can I use the internet to help me with my math homework? What happens if I type 'what is 15 x 9'?"

"You cannot use this for your math homework," he says with a laugh. "What does it say about sea breezes?"

I read, "A sea breeze is wind that blows from a large body of water toward or onto a landmass." I turn to Dad and say, "So, the wind that blows from the ocean to the land?"

"That's right," he says.

"But it doesn't say anything about rain," I say.

"Why don't you type in a different question into the search box," he suggests.

I sit for a moment with my hands frozen on the keyboard. My brain feels overloaded, but all of a sudden, I know what to type. "Do sea breezes cause storms," I say out loud as I type it into the search box. Bam! The internet does it again and comes up with an answer.

I read, "As the sea breeze moves inland, it causes clouds to form, and if the moisture in the air is high enough, showers or thunderstorms will develop. This typically happens during peak heating." I turn to Dad again. "Does peak heating mean the hottest part of the day, like the afternoon?"

"Sure does," he replies.

"So let me get this straight," I say, "the sea breeze pushes onshore and can create afternoon thunderstorms." We sit quietly for a moment as I try to make sense of it all. Dad just stares at me with a goofy but proud look on his face. Finally, I say, "Do we live closer to the coast?"

"Sure do," he says.

"Do you think the sea breeze could be a reason why the totals are always different?" I ask.

He nods.

"Maybe storms just haven't formed yet when the sea breeze is over our house, but by the time it is over the school, it's raining. In that scenario, our gauge would be empty but the school gauge wouldn't be," I say.

He nods again while taking another sip.

"Let's look at radar this afternoon to see where the storms form and how they move," I say.

"Sounds like a great plan," he says proudly.

18 Bonding Brothers

Robbie

As we walk the few blocks to the old football field, Daniel and I pass the ball back and forth, never dropping it.

“So, how’s school going?” Daniel asks while tossing the ball to me.

I stretch to catch it using only one hand. I pull it into my chest, and the crowd goes wild. Well, the crowd in my head does. “It’s fine,” I answer as I toss the ball back.

"Make any new friends?" he asks.

"Yeah, Emilio is pretty cool. He's the one that told me about this park."

"I'm glad he did," he says. After several throws and awkward silence, he adds, "Hey, remember when Dad would take us to Stoney Park, and we'd throw the ball for hours?"

"And Dad would be so sore the next day," I say as we both laugh.

"It's his own fault," he says. "He's the one that came up with his own version of football where he never had to run, only throw the ball hundreds of times to us. Maybe we can play some 'Stoney Football' for old times' sake after we're done with your project. I'll play Dad's role, and you can be the receiver for both teams."

"That sounds great," I say. After more silence, I mutter, "I'm sorry."

"For what?" he asks while juggling the ball.

"For distracting Dad," I say quietly.

Daniel stops walking and kneels down to my height. "You didn't do anything wrong, and you don't need to apologize. Accidents happen," he says while looking me in the eyes.

"I know, but he was driving because of me. If I just listened to you, I wouldn't have gotten hurt and wouldn't have needed to go to the hospital," I say while holding back tears.

"Kids get hurt and break bones sometimes. I did several times. It happens. You'll do stupid stuff again. It's not your fault he ran that red light," he says.

Daniel stands up while keeping his arm around my shoulders. We start to walk as he says, "I'm sorry if you thought I blamed you for any of it. I certainly don't."

"I blame myself," I say as a tear drops off my chin.

"Well, Grandma, Dad, and I don't blame you at all," he says, "and you shouldn't either. You're the family MVP, Most Victorious Prankster," he jokes while tightening his grip around my shoulders and messing up my hair.

"I got it from you," I say as I wiggle out of his grip.

"We got it from Dad," he says as he forces a hug on me. I give in and hug back.

19 Week of Observations

Julie

Just like that, another school week is almost complete. Each morning, I nail my weather reports. This morning I decide to try something new to keep my reports interesting. As I walk to the front of the class while holding the school's rain gauge, I say, "Can I please have an assistant?"

Several kids immediately raise their hands, including Robbie and Mary Sue. In that moment, I realize how comfortable I now feel in front of my classmates. All eyes are on me and my knees aren't buckling, my voice isn't shaking, and I actually enjoy being front and center. Robbie and I lock eyes as he whispers, "Pick me, pick me."

"Robbie, will you please help me take this morning's rainfall report?" I say in my best teacher voice. He is out of his seat and next to me before I even finish my sentence.

"Of course, Meteorologist Julie," he says in his perfect news anchor voice. "What do we have here? It appears to be a rain gauge that can hold several inches. Is that correct?"

"Sure is, Robbie." I answer as if we practiced this skit. "I'd like you to tell the class how much rain water is in the inner tube. You can tell by reading the ruler etched on the side of the cylinder."

"You mean this ruler here?" he says as he points to the inner tube.

"That's the one," I answer.

Robbie squats down to peer into the rain gauge. He makes a puzzled expression, turning back to the class so he can get a few laughs. His acting is so good I almost start laughing, but I manage to hold it together.

"I'd say 0.31 inches. Is that right?" he asks.

"That's correct. Want to guess how much fell at my house?" I ask.

"That exact amount," he confidently guesses.

"None," I say. "Not a drop."

"How can that be?" he asks.

"Well, yesterday's storms formed pretty much right over the school and then moved inland. The storm never passed over my house," I explain.

"Fascinating," Robbie says. "Are the reports between your house and the school always different?"

"I'm glad you asked, Robbie. I now have nearly two full weeks of rainfall measurements at both school and my house, and they have never received the same amount of rain. The more observations I take, the more questions I have about rainfall variability."

At this moment, I realize I just lost my audience.

"Julie," Ms. Clarke says, "why don't you explain what rainfall variability means?"

"I'd love to know," Robbie says while rubbing his chin.

I feel myself getting nervous, and I drop the rain gauge full of water all over the floor. My heart starts racing, and I turn bright red.

Robbie quickly grabs a roll of paper towels and starts soaking up the spilt water.

"Good thing we already took that reading, Meteorologist Julie," he says as the class laughs.

I take a deep breath and lock eyes with Robbie. He turns his back to the class so only I can see his face. He says softly, "It's okay. You got this."

My heart stops racing, and I say, "Rainfall variability refers to the differences in rainfall across an area." I take another deep breath. "For example, even though I live close to school, that doesn't necessarily mean when it is raining here that it will be raining at my house."

Wanting to stay a part of the skit, Robbie asks, "How can that be? You live so close to the school."

"I asked that same question. It turns out the weather is always changing. Storms are forming and falling apart constantly, which can result in different rain amounts, even across a small area. The more observations we take, the more questions we can answer."

"Boy, I sure would like to help and have one of these rain gauges at my house," Robbie says.

"Thank you Julie and Robbie," Ms. Clarke says as she walks to the front of the classroom. "You're absolutely right. The more of us that contribute to the daily weather puzzle, the more we can learn about weather."

Robbie and I look at each other and can't help but laugh. I'm so glad I chose him to be my assistant. Mary Sue wouldn't have been nearly as fun and would be mad I spilt water on her.

20 Flashback Friday

Robbie

Julie and I just made a touchdown followed by an extra point! It's like I could read her mind and knew just what she needed me to say during her weather report. Even Ms. Clarke loved it.

As we walk back to our desks, Ms. Clarke says, "Now that we all have our critical thinking caps on, I'd like everyone to pull out a blank sheet of paper for a Flashback Friday assignment."

Mary Sue's hand shoots up immediately.

"Yes, Mary Sue," Ms. Clarke says.

"Do you want us to tell you about our absolute favorite memory? I have a lot of them so it's going to be hard to choose just one, but maybe I should write about my recent haircut," she says.

"Or you could write about that time you watched Julie and me give an awesome weather report," I say to her as she pretends to ignore me.

"I'm sure you have tons of wonderful memories to share, Mary Sue, and maybe what I ask you to share today will be one of those experiences," Ms. Clarke says with a smile.

"Now class," she continues, "you have been working hard on your science projects, and with Science Night next week, you need to start organizing your thoughts and forming a conclusion. I'd like you to think about your research and what it was like to conduct an experiment. Then, write a paragraph or two about your experience and what you have learned."

I pull out a blank sheet of paper as Ms. Clarke walks back to her desk and sits down. I look around the silent classroom. Some kids are already writing while others look completely lost, some even terrified. Julie is already on her second paragraph. How is that even possible?

Mary Sue breaks the silence and says, "That was an easy assignment, Ms. Clarke."

"I'll take that as you're all done, Mary Sue. Let's remain quiet for those who are still working," Ms. Clarke says.

Finally, I write “Operation Field Goal Kick” at the top of my paper and look around the classroom again. I close my eyes and take a deep breath. For some reason I can’t get Mary Sue’s comment about sharing your favorite memory out of my head. Maybe it’s because spending the day with Daniel at the park, field goal kick after kick, is one of my favorite memories. I open my eyes and start writing about how we found Daniel’s field goal kick sweet spot.

21 Fan Favorite

Julie

At recess, I find Gracy on the swings and tell her about my morning weather report. “It was awesome! Robbie played the role as my assistant perfectly,” I say as I hop on a swing, quickly pumping my legs to get in sync with her.

“Aren’t you glad you didn’t trade jobs with Mary Sue and Robbie?” she asks as she slows her swinging speed.

There, we are perfectly in sync now.

"Absolutely!" I answer. "If I traded, I don't know what my science project would be. How is your dog feeding experiment going?" I ask.

"Well, it turns out, a dog doesn't care about the color of a bowl when it comes to eating. They will eat out of anything, and I mean anything!" she says.

"That sounds about right," I agree.

"However," she says while lifting her chin and holding up her pointer finger, "they do care about their water bowl color."

"Really? Do tell," I say.

"Yup, my research shows they prefer water in lighter colored bowls. I'm not sure exactly why, but if given the option, they almost always go for the lighter bowl," she says confidently.

"Fascinating," I say. "I can't wait to see your poster at Science Night."

"Oh, it will be colorful," she says. "I might not win first place, but I'll surely get the Fan Favorite Award. Who doesn't love dogs?" she says.

"Fan Favorite?" I ask.

"Yep," she says. "My teacher told us that every student who comes to Science Night will get to vote once for their favorite project. You just can't vote for yourself. At the end of the night, they hand out awards, including the one with the most student votes."

"Oh, that's almost better than winning first place," I say.

"What about you?" Gracy asks. "How is your project going?"

"Great," I say. "My dad is going to help me on my poster this weekend. I mainly just need to sort through the hundreds of pictures Clara took over the past two weeks and figure out which ones to include on my board."

"I don't mean to interrupt this boring conversation," Mary Sue says popping out from behind us, "but did you say there will be a Fan Favorite Award?"

"That's right," Gracy says. "What's your project topic?"

"Oh, no, no no. I can't tell you," Mary Sue says as she shakes her head and strokes her shorter hair. "It's going to be a surprise and certainly win the popularity award."

“It’s not a popularity award, Mary Sue,” I say as Gracy and I laugh. “People aren’t going to vote for your project just because it’s yours.”

“Yeah, okay Julie,” she says as she turns and walks away.

“Nice haircut, Mary Sue!” Gracy hollers. Then she leans towards me and whispers, “I just don’t understand that girl, but my mom says everyone deserves kindness.”

“Maybe your compliment is just what she needs,” I say.

22 The Home Stretch

Robbie

As we approach the school week finish line, the classroom is buzzing. Emilio and I are already talking about our weekend plans when Ms. Clarke says, "I know the bell is about to ring, but I need everyone to quiet down for one more announcement. Your posters are due on Monday so please work on them over the weekend."

With all eyes on Ms. Clarke, the school bell rings. Everyone stays frozen in their seats until she gives us the official nod that we can leave. I hop out of my desk and sprint toward the door. "No running!" Ms. Clarke says as I turn the corner out of our classroom. I slow my pace but remain in the lead.

My fast pace gets me to the bus loop first, and buses are already lined up. It's like the bus drivers are ready to start their weekend too.

"Hi Mr. Tony," I say as I climb onto the bus.

"What's going on, Robbie?" he says as he gives me a fist bump.

A few seconds later, Emilio huffs up the bus steps, fist bumps with Mr. Tony, and plops down next to me. "Man, I can't believe our posters are due Monday," he says to me shaking his head. "I still have so much to do."

"Like what?" I ask.

"Just a little research, a quick experiment, and an award winning poster," he says as he laughs.

"Way to wait until the last second, man," I say. "I just need to finish up my poster by adding a few drawings. Daniel and I had so much fun kicking field goals last weekend, we forgot to take pictures."

"Is he coming to Science Night with you?" Emilio asks.

"Says he wouldn't miss it," I answer. "My grandma will be there too. Is your family coming?"

"Yup, even my sisters," he says as he rolls his eyes. "If you need help with your drawings, just let me know. I love to draw. It's kind of why I'm behind on my project."

"Thanks. Maybe we can work on our projects at my house," I say as the bus turns on my street. "I'll ask my grandma and give you a call tomorrow."

"Sounds good," he says.

As soon as I get inside, I can smell Grandma's cooking. "Hey Grandma, what are you making?" I yell as I walk through the door.

"Your favorite," she hollers back.

"Spaghetti?" I say as I walk into the kitchen.

"Your other favorite," she says as she pulls me in close for a hug. "Happy Friday, Love."

I take a big whiff. "Banana bread," I say.

"That's right. Breakfast for the weekend," she says.

"Or a pre-dinner snack," I joke.

Just then we hear the front door open. "It's finally the weekend!" Daniel yells.

I run into the living room and jump up to give him a chest bump. After I find my balance I say, "I need to finish up my poster this weekend. Want to help?"

"Sure but not until you see this," he says as he pulls out a red and blue football jersey. "I made the football team!"

"Awesome!" I say as Grandma comes walking into the room. "Look Grandma, he made the football team."

"That's wonderful," she says.

"How about I wear it to Science Night and hold my football? It will be like I'm an extension of your poster," he says.

"Perfect! I'll even draw you on the poster wearing your new jersey," I say.

23 Science Night

Ms. Clarke

Science Night is my favorite night of the school year. The gymnasium is bright and full of proud students, families, and teachers. I love walking around the tables, hearing each child describe his or her project with such enthusiasm.

“Ms. Clarke,” Mary Sue calls as she waves me over, “this is my mom.”

As I walk toward them, I notice Mary Sue is the spitting image of her mother. Not a hair out of place, perfectly pleated skirt, and an indescribable confidence.

“Nice to meet you,” I say. “Mary Sue takes a lot of pride in her school work. You must be proud.”

“Of course. I make sure all her T’s are crossed and I’s are dotted,” Mary Sue’s mother says.

“Mary Sue,” I say turning towards her, “can you tell me about your project?”

“Absolutely!” She says. “Remember when I got my haircut?”

“How could I forget?” I say with a smile.

“Well, I kept my cut hair and divided it into six segments,” she says while pointing to her poster. “Then, every night I washed each clump of hair with shampoo and conditioner, using the same combination for each clump, to see which brand would leave hair the softest and shiniest.”

“How did you determine the results?” I ask.

"I conducted a nightly survey with my family. They would vote on which hair looked and felt the best," she explains.

"I'm impressed with your commitment to this project. Not many would cut their own hair for Science Night. Nicely done, Mary Sue," I say as she raises her chin proudly.

"This is valuable information," Mary Sue's mother says while avoiding eye contact with me. "Much more useful than knowing what color bowl a dog prefers."

"Ms. Clarke," Mary Sue interrupts while giving her mother an uncomfortable look, "can I use my fan favorite ticket to vote for my own project?"

"You can vote for any project other than your own. Why don't you look around and ask your classmates about their work?" I say gently.

"Ok," she says as she turns to walk away.

Not wanting to spend another moment with her mother, I excuse myself. “I think I’ll check out some other posters as well. It was nice meeting you,” I say to no reply.

Just then, Principal Diaz says into the microphone, “Good evening students. Judging results will begin in a few minutes so if you haven’t placed your fan favorite vote yet, please do so now. Good luck to all of you.”

“Hi, Ms. Clarke,” Robbie says. “Would you like to check out my poster?”

“Of course, Robbie,” I say. “By the way, your write-up on Friday was fantastic. It sounds like you and your brother had a great time at the old football field.”

“It was awesome!” he says while waving his brother over. “He’s on the high school football team.”

“It’s nice to meet you. Daniel, right?” I say.

“Yes, ma'am,” Daniel says with a football tucked under his arm.

Just then Julie walks up and places her fan favorite ticket in Robbie’s voting box.

“Thanks, Julie,” he says.

“I like your poster. You did a great job,” she says.

“Did you draw these pictures, Robbie?” I ask.

“Sure did,” he says, “with a little help from Emilio.”

"Well, they look great," I say.

"Those boys worked real hard this weekend," an older lady says as she walks toward us. "They nearly ate everything in my pantry."

"You must be Robbie's grandmother. I'm Ms. Clarke, his teacher," I say.

"And I'm Julie," Julie adds.

"I've heard wonderful things about both of you," she says.

"Grandma," Robbie mutters under his breath as he elbows her gently.

Principal Diaz's microphone cuts back on, and she says, "The results are in!" All the children squeal with excitement, and Julie scampers back to her poster.

As I walk to the stage, Principal Diaz goes on and on about the three different judges. One child impatiently mumbles, "Who won already?"

"And now for the awards," Principal Diaz finally says to a cheering crowd as she passes the microphone to me.

"Good evening everyone," I say. "Students, you should be so proud of yourselves. You all did a fantastic job. You've also been very patient tonight. I won't keep you waiting any longer. Let's get to the first award!"

"The Problem Solver Award goes to 5C's Gracy for her project on whether dogs have a bowl color preference. Originally, her experiment only included food bowl preference, but when she realized color didn't matter in that case, she shifted gears and tested their water bowl color preference. Way to reassess things, Gracy!"

The crowd cheers as Gracy hurries to the stage. Principal Diaz hands Gracy her award as I proceed.

“The next award is the Fan Favorite Award,” I say as children cross their fingers and fidget in anticipation. Robbie and I lock eyes as I say, “Congratulations to 5B’s Robbie for his field goal kick accuracy project.”

Robbie doesn’t move, and his brother gives him a nudge. He slowly starts walking toward the stage as his classmates pat him on the back. My eyes tear up as he approaches Principal Diaz, who hands him his award.

Robbie walks over to me and says, “Can I say something?”

“Certainly,” I say as I hand him the microphone.

The room is the quietest it’s been all night with all eyes on him. He finally says, “I’m sure none of you could tell, but I was really nervous at the beginning of the year. Starting at a new school with no friends was really scary." He pauses with the microphone still close to his mouth and a silent crowd. "Thankfully, I got a great teacher and quickly made new friends. It's actually been a really amazing year already," he says as the crowd cheers.

"One last thing," he adds, "I want to say thank you to my brother and Grandma. I couldn't have had this great of a start without you two, and Daniel, let's go play some 'Stoney Football' to celebrate."

His brother yells, "Heck yeah!" as the crowd roars even more.

Robbie hands me the microphone and makes his way down the stage. As I watch him walk through the crowd, high fiving any willing participant, I feel no need to talk or break this celebration. I stand still with a big goofy smile on my face, just listening to the crowd celebrate this wonderful boy.

Finally, the crowd quiets and looks at me. I discreetly wipe a tear from my cheek and say, "Our final award of the night is the Super Scientist Award. The winner of this award used science, technology, and math to collect and analyze data. This student made learning fun by asking questions and creatively sharing knowledge with others."

I see Robbie patting Julie on the back as she shakes her head in denial. I feel a lump in my throat, and my eyes tear up again as I try to keep my voice steady.

"5B's Julie researched rainfall variability by taking daily observations at both her house and this school, even on weekends. Julie, will you please come to the stage and accept your award?"

The crowd cheers as the once shy girl proudly walks to the stage and shakes Principal Diaz's hand and receives the Super Scientist Trophy. She walks over to me and gives me a hug.

"Would you like to say anything?" I whisper.

"Yes please," she says in a soft voice as she looks me right in the eyes and takes the microphone.

"I'd like to say thank you to you, Ms. Clarke. You helped me see that I can be a leader even though I'm only in fifth grade. I've gained a confidence I've never felt before at school, only at home. I know it's all because you encouraged me to do something different and new."

Tears break through and stream down my face as she gives me another hug.

"Lastly," she says as she turns back to the crowd, "I wouldn't have received this award without my little sister, Clara, who took the best pictures, and you can see them on my poster."

Through the cheers I hear a sweet voice yell, "Photos by Clara!"

Watching students cheer for one another brings me such joy. The twinkle in their eyes and humbleness to their smiles is why I enjoy working with children.

Throughout the remainder of the night, I have several more pleasant conversations with students and their families.

As the crowd dwindles, Principal Diaz says, “You did great tonight, Ms. Clarke. Your students really respect you and each other.”

“Thank you. It’s going to be a great school year,” I say beaming with pride.

The school year continues in…

The Chronicles of Ms. Clarke's Class

BATTLING BOTS

ACKNOWLEDGEMENTS

To my children, Hayden and Sidney.
This book wouldn't exist without the two of you. I have learned so much by watching you both tackle this wild world in your own unique ways.

To my husband, Brion Packett.
You have shown me success doesn't have to be measured by fancy job titles or promotions. Achievements come in all different sizes.

And to all my family, friends, and co-workers who have contributed to the making of this book. This includes, but is not limited to:

Ann & Rick Hunter
Holly Van Hoy
Carrie Grebenc
Connie McClanahan
MacKenzie Fulmer
Emily McGraw
Rebecca Davidson
Jennifer Morales

You will always be part of the PackAttack family.

Thank you!

ABOUT THE AUTHOR

Julie Packett is a woman, wife, mother, sister, daughter, spreadsheet addict, number enthusiast and weather nerd. After graduating with a Bachelor's Degree in Atmospheric Science, she became a meteorologist and quickly discovered her passion for educating children about weather safety. As a woman in the male dominated STEM field, she realized how influential her talks were for young girls when a female student dressed as a meteorologist on Career Day. She hopes this book can reach more children and encourage them to go after their own dreams, no matter how big or small.

ABOUT THE ARTIST

MacKenzie Fulmer is an illustrator and designer based in Kansas City, Missouri, who is passionate about humor and fashion. She studied Illustration at the Kansas City Art Institute and now pursues her goal of becoming an Art Director. When she is not making people laugh with her cartoons, she paints still lifes and landscapes.

Made in the USA
Columbia, SC
16 April 2021